The Story of the KAKAPO

PARROT OF THE NIGHT

Story by
Philip Temple

Illustrated by
Chris Gaskin

Hodder & Stoughton
AUCKLAND LONDON SYDNEY TORONTO

For Julika and Katya (P.T.)
For Badri and Sunanda (C.G.)

Introduction

Kakapo is the name given by the Maori to the large, flightless night parrot that they found in New Zealand's forests over a thousand years ago. Then, the kakapo lived all over New Zealand. Now, the only birds left are those that have been taken from their endangered homes in Fiordland and Stewart Island to the safety of Little Barrier and Codfish Islands. The number of kakapo was first reduced by Maori who hunted them and burned or cut down the forests where the birds lived. But the worst times for the kakapo came after Europeans began settling in New Zealand 150 years ago. Large areas of forest were cleared for farms, and meat-eating animals, such as stoats and cats, were brought to New Zealand. These animals found kakapo easy to kill. For many thousands of years kakapo had lived without such enemies. Surrounded by them the bird soon began to die out.

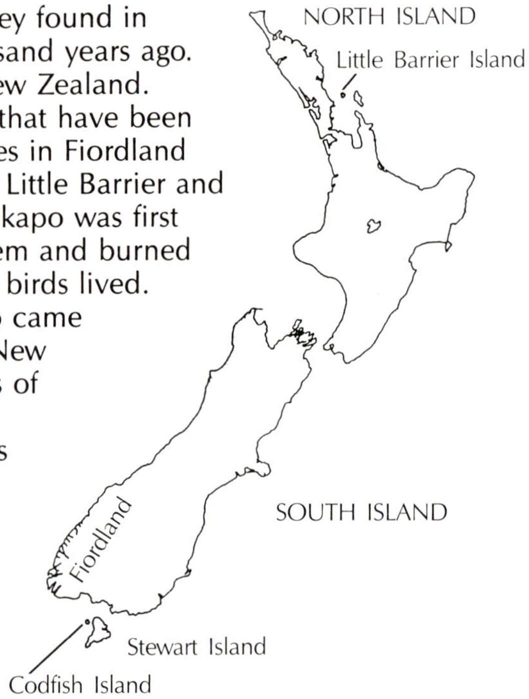

The kakapo was given the scientific name *Strigops habroptilus* by British scientist George Gray in 1845. It grows up to 60 centimetres in length and is the heaviest parrot in the world. Some males weigh as much as 3.5 kilograms. No one knows why the kakapo lost its power to fly or is active mostly at night. Perhaps it grew this way to evade ancient enemies, such as the now extinct giant eagle. The kakapo's special feature is that at mating time it booms and displays like a bower bird. No other bird in New Zealand does this, nor does any other parrot or flightless bird in the world.

The Story of the Kakapo describes the lives of kakapo that grew up on Stewart Island and the efforts being made to save the bird from dying out. We have called our kakapo Kairaki and Tutueka, Maori names for precious kinds of greenstone.

One warm February, Tutueka laid three eggs in the cosy nest she had made among the dry roots of an old rata tree. She had cushioned the nest's floor with powdered wood and feathers from her breast, leaving a patch of bare skin which warmed the eggs.

After the eggs were hatched, Tutueka worked hard. For months she cared for the chicks by herself, searching the bush and scrub for nourishing food. She even climbed high in rimu trees to collect autumn berries. The chicks were often left alone. But they grew strong under Tutueka's care, especially her first-hatched cock bird, Kairaki.

Early on a winter morning, Tutueka set out as usual to gather food for her chicks. They were now fully grown and she was tired and thin from many months of feeding and caring for them. Again she climbed high to gather the last wrinkled berries in a rimu tree.

Tutueka looked down suddenly as her chicks began growling and hissing. A hungry cat had found them. It sprang amongst them as they played outside their old nest. In a moment, two were dead. Only Kairaki escaped. He scrambled away as the cat ate its first victim. At the top of the rimu tree, Tutueka froze in fear. All her efforts had been wasted.

When he was driven from his home by the terrifying cat, young Kairaki roamed in search of a place of his own. He had learned he must often travel far to find the plants he needed. As he searched, other kakapo warned him away from their own ranges.

Kairaki wandered for a long time before he found an empty range with plenty of food. His new home was a high and wild place where the moonlight glinted on barren white rocks and hills rose up like the twisted roots around his old nest.

Kairaki explored every corner of his home range. He found out where the best fruiting trees were and which plants had the tastiest roots or richest bulbs. As time passed he grew to know when his favourite food plants were at their best. With his massive beak, he became expert at chewing and squeezing the juices from grasses and leaves. At grubbing out roots. At picking berries, nipping buds, gnawing bark, plucking flowers. And very carefully stripping seeds from stalks.

Kairaki grew fat and glossy and handsome. As the years went by, it didn't bother him to live almost always alone.

Every winter the great westerly gales came, bending the tallest trees. The scrub on the hilltops was shaped by the force of the wind. Deluges of rain flooded the creeks and washed away the last flowers and berries. It was the hardest time for Kairaki, when he could feed only on grass and tussock to keep himself alive.

In winter, Kairaki liked to roost on branches just below the ridge-tops, where he could catch most sun as he slept. But when the gales came he was forced to seek shelter in whatever dry and sheltered hollow he could find. There he waited until the worst was past, fluffing out his feathers to keep warm.

Kairaki was now about ten years old. As a new spring and summer came, all his favourite food plants grew and blossomed better than usual. He felt the urge to eat more and sensed that he would need much strength to survive the season of long twilights ahead.

Before the longest day, Kairaki left his home range and walked a long distance to a wide and open hilltop. He had been there two years before, attracted by eerie booming sounds in the night. He had seen other males dancing in the moonlight.

Females had come from the shadows to be with those males who boomed and danced the best. Now Kairaki felt it was his turn to mate. From what he had seen and learned, he shaped dancing and booming places for himself and cleared tracks to join them.

Kairaki dug three shallow bowls in the ground to reflect the sound of his booming. His favourite bowl was against a bank. It helped to project the booms far out into the night. Slowly he developed his booming, competing with other males nearby. Sometimes he screeched in warning to those who ventured too close. At first he boomed for only a short time.

By the middle of summer Kairaki was booming thousands of times a night under the warm starlit sky. The effort was so great that he lost most of the extra weight he had put on in the spring.

Between each spell of booming, Kairaki paused and listened for the low answering call of a female. It seemed as if it would never come.

Very early one morning, Kairaki's booming was rewarded. A smaller kakapo walked slowly from the bushes by his favourite bowl. The two birds called to each other and Kairaki began rocking gently from side to side. Instinctively he began to repeat what he had learned at the mating time two years before. He raised and lowered his colourful wings like a big, basking butterfly. He danced slowly backwards and forwards until he was certain that the young female was ready to mate.

When the mating season was over, Kairaki walked back to his home range. He was worn out. He had lost about a third of his weight and his feathers had begun to moult. For all his hard work during three months of booming, he had mated with only two females.

As he trekked over the hills, Kairaki sensed a great emptiness in the forest. He did not see the colours of other kakapo and heard no calls. Then he discovered a female wandering backwards and forwards in a clearing. She was one of the females Kairaki had mated with. She made noises of distress, stopping to touch broken shells and bloody feathers scattered among the leaves. They were all that was left of her chicks.

Suddenly, Kairaki saw fearsome eyes staring at him across the clearing. He remembered them from when he had been young. Alarmed, he turned back into the bush, merging with the leaves and branches. Behind him, he heard only terrible screeches.

When silence returned to the forest, Kairaki's sense of danger disappeared. Mistakenly, his ancient instincts still told him that the forest was safe for him.

After a good feed of totara leaves, Kairaki continued his homeward journey. He climbed out of a small valley, clambered over bare hilltop rocks and descended to the first trees of his home range.

As he reached out to cross from one tree-top to another he felt the branch shake beneath him. A dark shadow moved rapidly towards him. The fearsome eyes from the clearing were suddenly large, almost meeting his own. Kairaki let out a loud skraark – and jumped.

After he landed, Kairaki ran fast through the familiar forest of his home range. When he no longer sensed the cat, he slowed down and finally stopped. Again, all feeling of danger left him.

When daylight came, Kairaki dozed off in a roost he often used. It was a dry and sheltered spot among shrubs and low bushes. Here the sun lingered nearly all day and the only sound came from piping redpolls or trilling robins.

He woke suddenly when he heard a peculiar snuffling in his ear. He opened one eye and saw a strange creature panting by his side. It did not threaten him, but Kairaki dared not move a muscle. He sensed that if he did not move, perhaps he would not be seen. Then the smelly brown creature might go away and leave him in peace.

Kairaki was lifted into the air. He squawked and struggled, but his legs and head were firmly held. A white owlish face came close to his. Wide blue eyes examined him carefully and long white claws parted his feathers. He clamped one of the claws in his strong beak when a bright band was fixed around his leg. Then he relaxed when he no longer sensed danger.

Kairaki found himself placed in a dark burrow lined with familiar leaves and twigs. Most of these came from his favourite food plants. There was stillness and silence for a long time, and then a loud beating sound he had never heard before. He closed his eyes as he felt his burrow move and swing and lift. For the first time, Kairaki was flying.

Kairaki walked from his dark, rocking burrow to find himself in a place where the air was strangely warm and filled with new scents. The lush forest echoed with the calls of birds both familiar and new. Kairaki looked for something to eat. Many of the plants he could not recognise at all. Wearily, he set out to climb towards the top of a steep hill. He sensed it would be cooler up there and that he might find all the plants and rocks and cold starlit skies he knew so well.

Not far away, Tutueka also climbed the same hill. She had hatched many eggs since Kairaki had left her, but few of her chicks had survived. She too had been taken to this new land and, like Kairaki, had to become acquainted with a new home range. When the summer came again, perhaps she would hear booming among the sharp volcanic peaks. And perhaps her next brood of chicks would safely join the teeming seabirds and numberless, loud songbirds which lived here without the threat of savage teeth and claws.

Facts about the Kakapo

The diagrams on these pages serve as keys to the colour illustrations in this book.

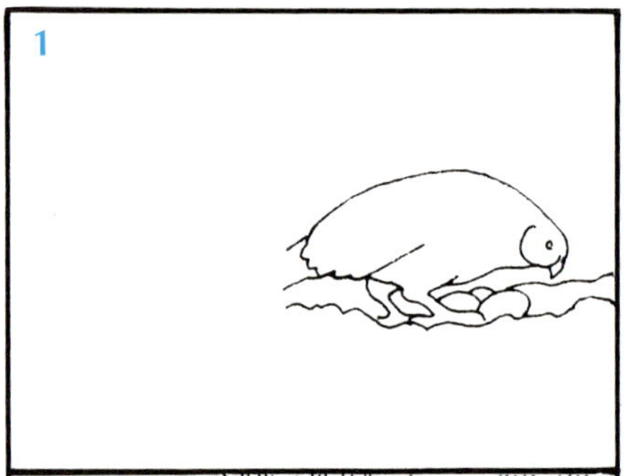

1 During late summer, female kakapo lay 2–4 eggs in natural holes in banks, at the base of trees, in old logs or under tussocks. Females care for eggs and chicks alone. Incubation takes about a month and chicks stay in the nest for about three months, until they are fully grown. It is thought that after leaving the nest, young birds stay with their mother until they are used to feeding and caring for themselves.

2 Though heavy and flightless, kakapo are very agile. With strong legs and feet they climb into the crowns of tall trees to collect fruit. Most of their activity occurs at night but it is not known if kakapo have better night-sight than other birds. Females are smaller and weigh less than males. Other animals depicted are a short-tailed bat (*Mystacina tuberculata*) [A], a possum (*Trichosurus vulpecula*) [B], and a rat (*Rattus rattus*) [C].

3 In most parts of New Zealand kakapo have died out after the arrival of European mustelids (stoats, ferrets and weasels) and dogs. The kakapo has not been able to cope with such enemies in a country previously free of meat-eating mammals. Kakapo have an attractive scent and spend most of their time on or near the ground so they are easily located. They are particularly vulnerable to attack when young because mothers leave chicks alone for long periods while collecting food. As kakapo do not raise chicks every year, regular killing by mammals causes a rapid decline in the bird's numbers. There are no mustelids on Stewart Island: wild cats were the greatest threat to the birds that lived there.

4 Adult kakapo live alone and need large home ranges with a variety of food plants. Male ranges are 15–30 hectares in area. Female ranges are larger — 35–50 hectares — probably because of the females' need to have plenty of food for their young. Ranges often overlap, male and female, and birds 'poach' on each other's territory. Sometimes kakapo announce their presence by screeching out ('skraarking') to others. This is a signal which helps to keep the birds apart.

Outside the breeding season kakapo do not often move from their home ranges, but are able to travel several kilometres in a night. They come to know large areas of country and where to find seasonal foods, even beyond their own usual ranges.

5 Kakapo take food from many plants, ranging from grass to forest trees, and eat many parts of plants: roots, rhizomes, bulbs, twigs, buds, leaves, leaf stems, flowers, flower stems, pollen cones, fruits, berries, seeds and bark. Their diet changes with each season as each food source becomes available. It may also vary from year to year.

6 Kakapo have lived in many different places, from the warm lowland forests of the North Island (in prehistoric times), to the sub-alpine areas of the Southern Alps. Stewart Island has a cool climate, with high rainfall and strong winds.

The kakapo's plumage helps the bird to survive. The kakapo has a down layer beneath its feathers, like a duck's. This natural duvet keeps the bird warm. The kakapo's feathers are soft, but it keeps them in good condition by grooming them with oil from a gland above its tail.

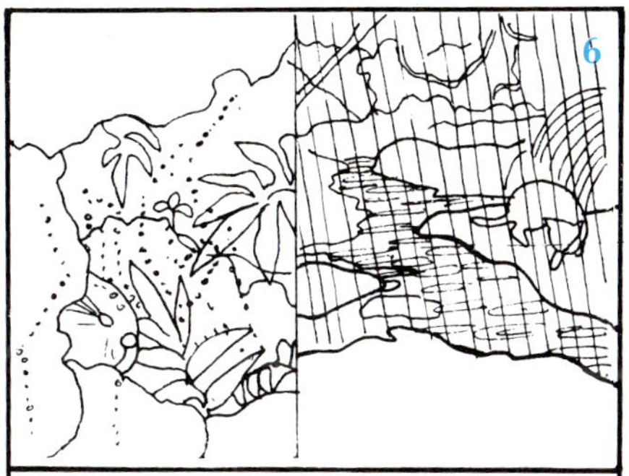

7 During the breeding season kakapo males make special calls ('booms') and displays to attract females. This is the only time that males and females come together. Males travel up to 6 kilometres to find the best display sites where they prepare tracks to join their booming and dancing places (a 'track and bowl system'). Tracks are 30–60 cm wide and males keep them clear by clipping plants at the sides. The tracks may extend for as much as 50 metres. Kakapo breed between December and March, but only in those years when there is enough food for raising chicks.

The kakapo is the only such 'lek' display bird in New Zealand. It is the only 'lek' display parrot and 'lek' flightless bird in the world.

The other bird in the picture is a Stewart Island brown kiwi *(Apteryx australis).*

8 Kakapo males make booms by inflating air sacs in their chest. Booms are like the sound made by blowing across the top of a large bottle. In each spell of booming the sounds slowly become louder and then fade away. The loudest booms can be heard at least a kilometre away and up to five kilometres away down wind. Males spend a great deal of time booming. They start about dusk and finish at dawn. One Stewart Island male was recorded as making 9000 booms during one night! A male may boom every night from mid-December to late March. Booming bowls (natural sound shells) are about 5 cm deep and 45 cm wide. (See also illustration on title page.)

9 A female is attracted to a male by his booming. The male's 'dance' display is probably needed to prepare the female for mating. A young and inexperienced male kakapo may attract no females. An expert and vigorous male may mate several times in one mating season.

10 Until birds were moved from Stewart Island there were more male than female kakapo. This may be explained by the fact that females are more easily caught by cats as they look after their young. Females also have a more demanding, and perhaps shorter, life caused by the strain of being 'solo parents'. No one knows how long kakapo normally live. Large parrots in other parts of the world may reach 60 or 70 years of age.

11 Kakapo cannot fly but are able to 'parachute' from trees, using their wings for balance and braking. Some reports suggest they are able to make steep glides, up to a distance of 50 metres. Their wings are also useful for balance when they are running.

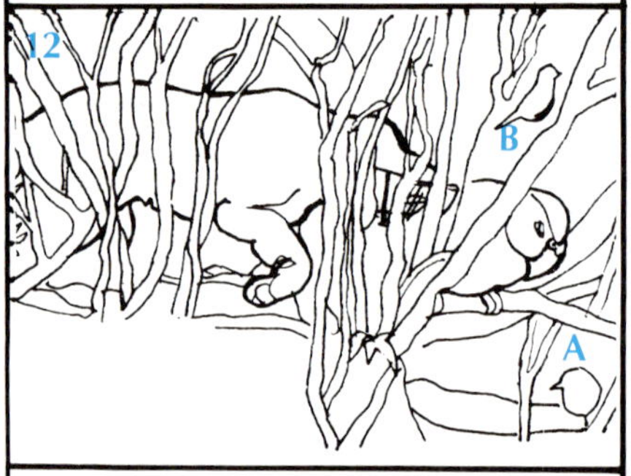

12 The kakapo's only form of self-defence is to become absolutely still and allow its barred and speckled feathering to act as camouflage. This worked well centuries ago when the kakapo's chief enemies were probably the giant eagle and other 'sight hunters'. Today this 'protection' is useless against mammalian hunters which rely on their sense of smell to track down prey.

Kakapo have a strong musky smell and Department of Conservation officers decided to use muzzled tracker dogs on Stewart Island to locate kakapo for study and rescue. Kakapo camouflage still works well in concealing the birds from humans!

The two small birds in the picture are the native bush robin (*Petroica australis*) [A], and the introduced redpoll (*Carduelis flammea cabaret*) [B].

13 The kakapo population on Stewart Island was being steadily destroyed by cats. To give kakapo a chance of survival the Department of Conservation airlifted all the birds that could be found to other islands which are free of their mammal enemies.

Captured kakapo are placed individually in foam-padded cages lined with familiar plants. The birds are transported by helicopter and plane as quickly as possible to minimise the shock and disturbance caused by capture and air travel.

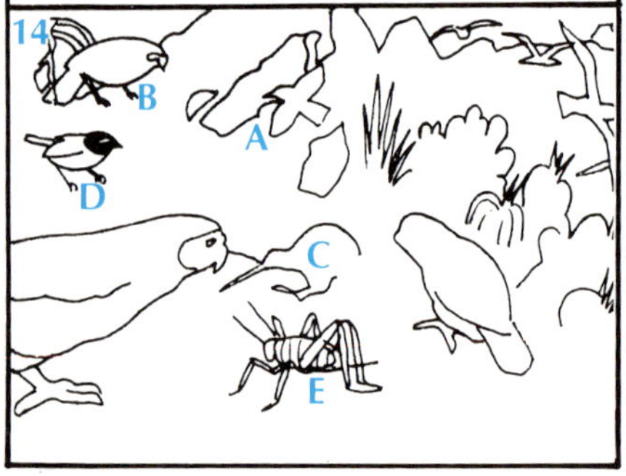

14 In 1982, 9 female and 13 male kakapo were transferred to Little Barrier Island in the Hauraki Gulf, and between 1987 and 1990, 9 females and 20 males were moved to Codfish Island, close to Stewart Island. A few kakapo may still remain on Stewart Island but the birds are now thought to be extinct in Fiordland.

Little Barrier was finally cleared of cats in 1980. Since then, threatened saddlebacks (*Philesturnus carunculatus*) [A] and kokako (*Callaeas cinerea*) [B] have been transferred there from the North Island mainland and have bred successfully. Kakapo on Little Barrier have boomed but have not yet bred successfully. The protection and feeding support given the kakapo there, and on Codfish Island, may well allow this unique bird its best chance of survival. Three male kakapo are being kept in captivity on Maud Island in the Marlborough Sounds for research into their breeding behaviour.

Also depicted are the North Island brown kiwi (*Apteryx australis mantelli*) [C], stitchbird (*Notiomystis cincta*) [D], and the giant weta (*Deinacrida heteracantha*) [E]. The birds silhouetted against the sky are seabirds, such as black and Cook's petrels.

Acknowledgements

For their help the author and artist extend their sincere thanks and appreciation to Hugh Best, Don Merton and Ralph Powlesland of the Department of Conservation, Wellington; Ron Scarlett of the Canterbury Museum, Christchurch; Rod Morris, Television New Zealand, and Otago Museum, Dunedin; and Ron Tindal and Andy Roberts of the Department of Conservation, Stewart Island.

The artist is especially appreciative of the generosity and humour of Phred, Wally, Nick and Wayne who managed to reveal the lighter sides of mudholes, persistent rain, sleet, cold and gales, and make the frustrations for an artist working at the south end of Stewart Island just bearable.